WHAT'S INSIDE THE CHRISTMAS TREE

DEDICATED TO THE SMILE ON YOUR FACE

XOXO THE AUTHOR

EVER HEARD OF THE CHRISTMAS TREE OF THE NORTH POLE?

IT'S TALLER THAN A BLUE WHALE

JUMPING FROM THE OCEAN FLOOR

IT'S WIDER THAN A BULKY BROWN BEAR STANDING ON ITS HIND FEET
AND WHAT'S INSIDE IS WONDER –
WAITING FOR ALL WHO WANT TO SEE

EVER HEARD OF THE CHRISTMAS
TREE OF THE NORTH POLE?
IT'S TALLER THAN A
SPECKLED GIRAFFE
MUNCHING LEAVES FROM WHENCE
THEY GROW

IT'S WIDER THAN A HERD OF GREY ELEPHANTS TRACKING FOOTFALLS TO THEIR MUD BATH

AND WHAT'S INSIDE IS A GIFT FOR ALL WHO CAN FIND THE PATH

WHAT'S INSIDE THE CHRISTMAS TREE
OF THE NORTH POLE?

SCURRYING INSIDE THE CHRISTMAS TREE
ARE MARVELOUS ANIMALS HAPPILY WORKING.
IT'S WHERE THEY TAKE THEIR TEA;
THE SNOWY OWL ,
CHIPMUNKS
AND SNOWSHOE BUNNY

IT'S WHERE THEY SLEEP SOUNDLY;

THE BIRDS,
BABY MICE
AND THE BEES

IT'S WHERE THEY SHARE A WORKSHOP;
THE FIREFLIES,
THE WOODCHUCKS
AND THE ARCTIC FOX

WHY ARE THE
MARVELOUS ANIMALS
INSIDE THE
CHRISTMAS TREE?

THEY FANCY COLLECTING LIGHT, SO THEY CAN SET IT FREE
THEY FORGE ,
FORAGE,
POLISH
AND PECK
ROUNDING UP AND TAKING CARE OF EVERY LITTLE SPECK

HOW CAN YOU BE CERTAIN
THE ANIMALS ARE TRULY WORKING?

LOOK FOR THE PINE NEEDLES SWAYING BACK AND FORTH
THEN YOU'LL KNOW THE MARVELOUS ANIMALS ARE
MOVING AROUND TO HELP THE EARTH;
THEY FORGE
FORAGE,
POLISH AND PECK
EVERY SINGLE PINE NEEDLE
UNTIL IT'S BRILLIANT AND RICH

AND GUESS WHAT ELSE
YOU MAY SPOT?

VIBRANT GREEN PINE NEEDLES FLYING ACROSS
THE SKY IN A JOYOUS TROT

WHEN THE SPRINKLES LAND, LISTEN FOR THE
RAT-A-TAT-TAT
AS THEY BLOOM TO CLEAN OUR AIR, WATER AND HABITATS

WHY DO THE MARVELOUS ANIMALS DO IT?
WHAT DO THEY GET?

THEY DO IT BECAUSE THEY KNOW THAT THERE IS
SEEN AND UNSEEN LIGHT
THAT ZIPS THROUGH THE AIR LIKE A WONDROUS KITE
AND THEY KNOW THAT ONE CANNOT EXIST WITHOUT THE OTHER~
THAT THE INSIDE AND OUT GO TOGETHER

HAVE YOU SEEN HOW LOVELY THE OUTSIDE
OF THE CHRISTMAS TREE IS DECORATED?
STICKY, SWEET CANDY,
SHINY ORNAMENTS
AND FRESH HOLLY
CAN KEEP OUR EYES
QUITE FASCINATED

YET, INSIDE THE CHRISTMAS TREE IS AN EVEN GREATER GOODIE ~
IT'S FULL OF A BRIGHTNESS, A JOY AND A LOVE
THAT CAN ONLY COME FROM ABOVE

FOR YOU SEE THE CHRISTMAS TREE OF THE NORTH POLE

LIVES

DIRECTLY

BELOW

THE NORTH STAR ~

IT KEEPS THE WORLD FROM BEING DARK

AND IT'S THE VERY SAME LIGHT THAT OUR ANCESTORS GAZED UPON

FOR THOUSANDS OF YEARS...

THE CHRISTMAS TREE HAS BEEN A PLACE FOR ALL TO GATHER
IN HARMONY, LAUGHTER AND CHATTER
SO THE MARVELOUS ANIMALS
FORGE,
FORAGE,
POLISH
AND PECK~
SIDE BY SIDE
UNTIL THEY CATCH THE LIGHT
IN A HUG
THEN
ON TIPPY TOES, THEY LIFT IT UP
TO THE NORTH STAR
SO IT CAN SHINE NEAR AND FAR

ARE YOU READY TO PEEK INSIDE?

YOU SEE, THE LIGHT FROM
THE NORTH STAR NEVER
EVER GOES AWAY.
IT TWINKLES IN THE NIGHT
AND THE DAY;
CRADLED WITHIN THE TREE,
PEACEFUL, COZY AND WARM,
BY MARVELOUS LITTLE
ANIMALS WHO WILL NEVER
LET IT BE BLOCKED BY ANY
DUST STORM

IS THERE ANYTHING ELSE INSIDE THE CHRISTMAS TREE?

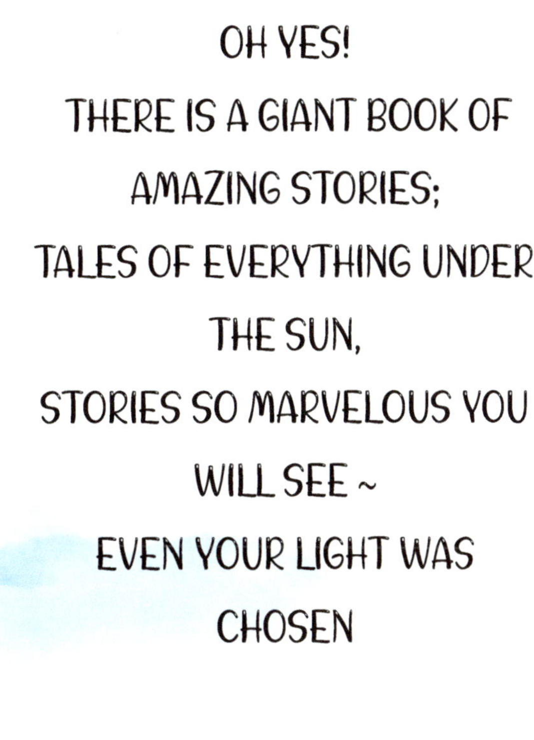

OH YES!

THERE IS A GIANT BOOK OF

AMAZING STORIES;

TALES OF EVERYTHING UNDER

THE SUN,

STORIES SO MARVELOUS YOU

WILL SEE ~

EVEN YOUR LIGHT WAS

CHOSEN

ONE STORY BEGINS LIKE THIS:

EVER HEARD OF THE CHRISTMAS TREE OF THE NORTH POLE?

IT'S

AS

TALL

AS YOU,

AS MIGHTY AS YOUR EMBRACE,

AS WIDE AS THE SMILE ON YOUR FACE

AND LIKE A RAY OF SUNLIGHT~

CAN ABOUND THE WORLD AND BRIGHTEN WITH A TOUCH OF GRACE

ARE THERE MORE STORIES AND GIFTS HIDDEN INSIDE THE CHRISTMAS TREE?

THEY ARE NOT HIDDEN, THEY'RE
INSIDE FOR YOU TO BEHOLD
WHEN YOU CHASE
THE UNBROKEN
CRISSCROSS BABY BRANCH
PROTECTED BY THE
SPARKLY
HEART
OF
GOLD

PEEK INSIDE TO LAY YOUR EYES UPON THE
LIGHT AND FOLLOW
AND YOU'LL DISCOVER THIS GRAND TREE
HAS NEVER BEEN HOLLOW

THEN GIVE THANKS EVERY DAY IN THIS MARVELOUS ADVENTURE;
AN AMAZING JOURNEY WHERE THE INSIDE AND OUT GO TOGETHER

CHECK OUT MORE BOOKS FROM THE AUTHOR!

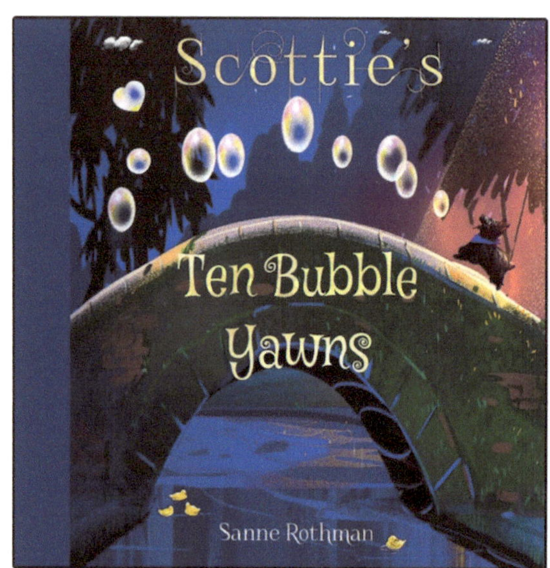

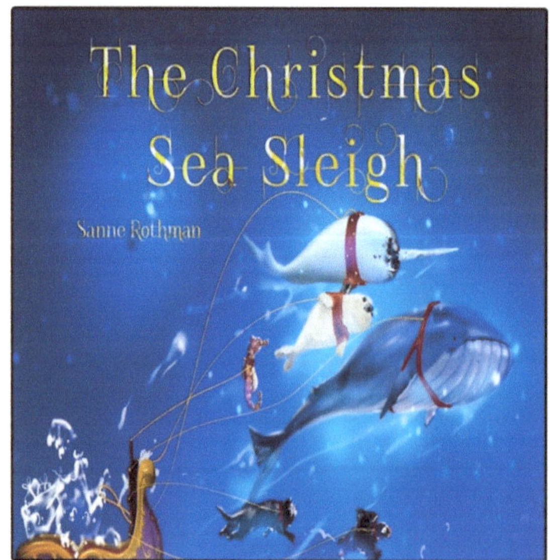

www.ingramcontent.com/pod-product-compliance
Lightning Source LLC
LaVergne TN
LVHW070206110826
845147LV00002B/512

* 9 7 8 1 7 3 6 1 2 5 1 2 0 *